The Deer in the Pasture

by DONALD CARRICK

GREENWILLOW BOOKS
A DIVISION OF WILLIAM MORROW & COMPANY, INC., NEW YORK

Library of Congress Cataloging in Publication Data
Carrick, Donald. The deer in the pasture.
Summary: When hunting season comes,
a deer who has become too friendly with
man must be frightened and driven away
for its own protection.
[1. Deer—Fiction]   I.   Title.   PZ7.C2345De
[E]   75-23193   ISBN 0-688-80023-8
ISBN 0-688-84023-X lib. bdg.

For the Dunbars

Each morning after milking,
Mr. Wakeman walked his cow herd
to pasture.

Late one summer he noticed a deer
watching the cows.

In a day or two the deer
joined the herd.
"He must be lonely, poor fella,"
said Mr. Wakeman.

The cows accepted him into the herd.
But sometimes he played too rough.

At evening milking time the deer
began to follow the cows toward the barn.

One evening the deer came inside
the barn. After that he came
each evening.

Mr. Wakeman's grandchildren
liked to feed the deer.
"He feels safe with us,"
Mr. Wakeman told them.
"If he didn't, his tail would
go up as a warning signal."

On the way home from school the children
stopped to watch the wild deer
grazing with the cows.

But as fall haying ended, other eyes
were watching the deer, too.
"Deer hunting season is coming,"
thought Mr. Wakeman.
"Something must be done to protect
that deer from being shot."

Mr. Wakeman called the game warden.
"This deer has learned to trust people.
Hunters won't know that he is so tame."
"You can't tie up a wild deer, and he'd
break out of any regular fence," answered
the warden. "But we can't let him be shot."

Before hunting season began,
the game warden and Mr. Wakeman
drove the deer to a place
far away from people and cows.

"He will find all the food he needs
around here," the warden said.
But the deer stayed close to the men.
"I was afraid of this," said Mr. Wakeman.
"He will follow us back for certain."

The warden pointed his gun
at the sky and fired.
It seemed cruel, but they had
to frighten the deer.

"He belongs in the wild," said the warden.
"It's the first time I've seen his tail up,"
said Mr. Wakeman.

Mr. Wakeman did no hunting that season.

MAY 2 5

MAY 3 0

JUN 0 2

SEP 2 8 2000

OCT 4

4

PRINTED IN USA

14406